JF Har

Walking
The Goldfish

MICHAEL HARDCASTLE

D1486371

Illustrated by
SAMI SWEETEN

HEINEMANN

William Heinemann Limited
Michelin House
81 Fulham Road
London SW3 6RB

Distributed in Australia by
the Octopus Publishing Group Australia (Pty) Ltd
22 Salmon Street
Port Melbourne
Victoria 3207
Australia

LONDON   MELBOURNE   AUCKLAND

First published 1990
Text © Michael Hardcastle 1990
Illustrations © Sami Sweeton 1990

ISBN 0 434 97667 9
Printed in Italy
by Olivotto

Chapter One

HARRY STROLLED RESTLESSLY round and round the room. He put his face close up to Cleo's but then moved on when she didn't even wink back at him. He took a book off a shelf and then put it straight back where it had been. He peered at the people in a photo as if they were strange animals in a zoo, even though he himself was one of those people in the silver-framed picture.

His father stood it for a few minutes. Then he said: 'Harry, sit down! You're driving me mad. And I want to watch this video in peace.'

'But I'm *bored*,' answered Harry.

'You can't be! You've got books and TV and all your friends in the village. You've got everything any boy needs to be happy and interested in life. It's *impossible* for you to be bored.'

'It's not impossible, and I *am* bored.'

His dad gave a deep groan and switched his gaze from the video. Fingering his moustache, he glanced round the room and spotted the goldfish bowl. 'Look,' he said, pointing, 'look at Cleo. What about her, eh? Now, she has every right to be bored. Nothing to do all day but swim round and round that bowl. Never sees anything new, unlike you. She's the one you ought to feel sorry for, Harry, not yourself.'

'I *do* feel sorry for her,' said Harry, jumping up to make faces at his goldfish again. But she didn't seem a bit interested in what he was doing, 'especially if she's as bored as I am. But what can I do about it?'

'Oh, *I* don't know – take her for a walk, or something.' His Dad grinned, but with his eyes still fixed on the screen.

Harry was suddenly delighted. 'Do you mean it, Dad? Can I really take Cleo for a walk?' He began to plan where they might go in the village.

'I said so, didn't I? Go on, get off with you – then you'll both stop being bored.' The video was showing pictures of funny-looking, flat-topped cars whizzing past each other like super-fast ants.

Harry wondered how to carry Cleo on her walk. She lived in a very large, heavy bowl that was hard enough just to lift. Then, in the kitchen, he remembered the see-through jug they put Cleo into when they changed the water in her bowl. It wasn't very big but it was easy to carry because it had a handle. Harry grinned to himself as he always did when he had a bright idea.

He lifted Cleo out of the bowl with a
net and put her into the jug with some
water. Then he looked across at his
father. But he was still watching the
same whizzing cars. 'Bye,' he called
from the back door. There was no reply.

5

Chapter Two

'Now, Cleo, this is our village,' he told
the goldfish. 'What do you think of it?
Do you like those nice houses over
there? And . . . oh yes, the school with
the paddling pool next to it?' He didn't
get a reply from her, either, but then he
didn't expect one.

'When Neil Hodges heard about you
he said *he* wanted a piranha. But his

Mum'll only let him have a hamster!
Hard luck. Now see that house there
with the purple door, that's where
stupid Jed lives. He's almost as nutty as
Kenny, his best friend. They're crazy,
those two.'

A ginger cat was sitting on the wall of
the next house. It was Boris. He
belonged to Mrs Lister, a neighbour
who didn't like small boys; fat cats were
her favourites. Boris was fascinated by
Cleo swimming around in the water and
he wanted a closer look. He sprang up
and, tail high, moved quickly towards
them.

Harry backed away. 'Go away,' he hissed at Boris. 'You've had your dinner. You always do at midday. Mrs Lister says so. She tells everyone what you eat.'

But Boris wouldn't go: he had his eyes on Cleo. He seemed to be drawn towards her like a magnet.

'Goldfish don't taste very good,' said Harry, hoping that was true. 'You wouldn't like Cleo at all.' He added, under his breath: 'And she *hates* you, Boris, and all cats.'

Suddenly, Boris began to mew
loudly, his gaze still fixed on Cleo.
Harry was alarmed. He feared the cat
was going to attack them. Just as he was
deciding where to run to, he spotted
Shark. That wasn't his real name but he
had so many teeth, and he moved so
swiftly and silently, he really was like a
shark. In fact, he was just an odd sort of
dog.

Harry whistled, something he was
good at, though not many people
seemed to want him to whistle. But

dogs always pricked up their ears when
they heard him. Shark didn't. His
interest was in Cleo and he even ignored
Boris. The cat didn't seem to notice
Shark's arrival because Cleo was still the
centre of his attention. They both stared
up at the see-through jug as Harry held
it up at shoulder-level. He was angry as
well as worried. This wasn't right at all:
dogs and cats should chase each other,
not join up to frighten a poor
defenceless little goldfish.

'Go AWAY!' he shouted more than once. But dog and cat simply circled round him, staring up at the jug as if it were a kind of TV show put on just for them. Now Harry looked round for real help in getting rid of Boris and Shark. It was then that Mr Tinker walked by.

'Starting a zoo, are you, Harry?' he asked, grinning. 'I know a budgie that's not wanted. You can have that to join your collection. Oh yes, and since Mrs Foster died her duck, Abigail has been like a lost soul. She'd be good for your little zoo, Harry. Needs company, I reckon.'

Harry didn't think it was at all funny. 'I'm just taking my goldfish for a walk, that's all, Mr Tinker. But Boris and Shark won't leave us alone. Can you send them away, please?'

'Oh, don't worry about them,' said the old man, waving his walking stick in the air. 'They'll soon get bored if they don't get what they want. And that's your fishy friend, I reckon. Come on, let's go and see Abigail.'

'I don't like ducks,' Harry pointed out, moving on beside Mr Tinker.

'They're greedy. The ones that live on the pond are. They eat enough bread to stock a bakery, my mum says.'

'Oh, you'll like Abigail,' promised Mr Tinker, swinging his walking stick round and round in his fingers like a juggler in a stage show. 'She's a bit sad at the moment, though. She's missing Mrs Foster who treated her just like one of the family. Practically lived in the kitchen, Abigail did. So you can cheer her up, Harry. You and your fishy friend.'

Harry wished Mr Tinker wouldn't keep saying that. It made Cleo sound like a joke. He guessed that Cleo herself didn't like to be called anyone's fishy friend. When he looked back he saw that Shark seemed to have lost interest in Cleo at last. He'd stopped for a long sniff at a gatepost in front of Mrs Simpson's bungalow. But Boris, tail high in the air, was still following them (and because Mr Tinker had a limp they weren't going very fast).

'Can't you get rid of Boris, please, Mr Tinker?' Harry asked politely. 'I think he wants Cleo for his dinner. I don't fancy that. He looks as if he's waiting for the right moment to pounce on her.'

Mr Tinker laughed. 'Old Boris wouldn't do that. Just wants to be pally.' But he shook his stick at the cat and Boris fled.

Chapter Three

Harry was glad to be able to lower the jug to a comfortable height. He peered in at Cleo. As she looked quite normal he couldn't tell whether or not she was enjoying the outing.

'Had her long?' asked Mr Tinker, pointing his twisted stick straight at her.

'Since my birthday. That was five weeks ago,' replied Harry. 'She was a present from my nan. She said a goldfish might calm me down.'

'Oh,' said Mr Tinker with a grin, 'a hot-blooded lad, are you?'

'How d'you mean?' Harry wanted to know.

'Oh, dashing here, dashing there, getting yourself into this and that. A real firework, always fizzing. Bit thoughtless, too. You know, acting first and thinking afterwards.'

'I don't think I'm like that,' Harry said calmly. 'I just like to be doing things, that's all.'

'Well, maybe Cleo needs somebody like you to liven her up,' said Mr Tinker. 'Must be boring being a goldfish. Hasn't got any tricks she can do, has she, to keep herself amused.

'She can wink,' Harry declared. 'That's very special.'

Mr Tinker paused. 'Can she?' He didn't look as though he believed that.

'Let's see, then.' He bent down to peer
into the jug as Harry held it up for him.
But Cleo flicked her tail and dived away
from him.

'Wink!' exclaimed Mr Tinker with a
louder laugh this time. 'She doesn't
wink for me.'

'You've got to be fast to see it,' Harry
explained.

'Oh, well, I'm not very fast at all,'
said Mr Tinker with a laugh. 'Anyway,
come on, you said you liked some
action. So let's meet Abigail. See if I can
get along faster than I usually do.'

Chapter Four

MR TINKER BEGAN to stride out so
briskly Harry had to hurry to keep up.
Cleo's jug was getting heavier all the
time. Harry wished he could put it
down and have a good rest. Maybe Cleo,
too, was ready to stay in one place for a
little while. To a fish as small as she
was, this must seem like a journey
round the world.

Mr Tinker turned into High Farm
Lane – and let out a yell. He raised his
stick high above his head, looking as if
he were going to attack somebody.
'Leave her alone, you devils!' he roared.
'Harry, you chase 'em away! Your legs
are younger than mine.'

Harry stared down the lane at the two geese which seemed to be playing a game with a duck, a duck that was even fatter than Boris. Abigail was quack-quack-quacking like a crazy radio programme. And she seemed to get louder when she saw Mr Tinker and Harry. The geese were rushing at her and all three birds were going round in circles. It was clear that Abigail didn't like this game at all. Abigail wanted to get away.

'They're tormenting her, dreadful creatures,' Mr Tinker was yelling. 'Go on, Harry, send 'em packing.'

He still had his stick raised but he made no move towards Abigail and the attacking geese. Carefully Harry placed Cleo's jug on a flat piece of ground by the side of the lane. He didn't know what he was going to do, but he wanted to help Abigail; those big geese were being really rotten to her.

Harry spread his arms wide and then charged towards the birds, yelling as loud as he could. He was yelling his war cry: 'Yah-yah-yah-yah!' Once, on TV, he'd seen a rugby team perform their special war cry; and then they'd won the game they were playing. He didn't have any fear that the birds would turn and attack him. In any case, Mr Tinker was behind him with his stick held high. With the old man behind him he would come to no harm. 'Go on, Harry, get at 'em!' Mr Tinker shouted.

Harry was like an aeroplane coming in to land. Swooping and turning, swooping and turning. The birds scattered at once. One goose ran to the right, one to the left, in a kind of swerving run, hissing and snapping, hissing and snapping. They looked mad at him. But they went, flapping their wings; they went down the lane and over a low wall and into a yard. Abigail had flopped down on her tummy, looking worn out. She probably was. She gave Harry a soft sort of look as if she were trying to say thank you.

'Well, you did a good job there, son,' said Mr Tinker. He hadn't moved from where Harry had left him. He pushed his cap back to wipe some sweat off his forehead with the back of his hand. 'You sure sent 'em packing.'

Harry studied Mr Tinker's face and noticed that it was lined and crumpled. 'Were you scared of those geese, Mr Tinker?' he asked.

'Oh, I reckon I was, Harry. Can't stand the racket they make. Geese is nasty creatures when they get their dander up, like that pair. Geese can do a lot of damage, geese can.'

'What's their dander?' Harry wanted to know.

'Er, temper, I suppose. Yes, temper. Geese have nasty tempers. But you knew how to deal with them, Harry. I knew you would. That's because you've got hot blood, too, like your nan said. You weren't scared at all, were you? I'm proud of you. And Abigail here is grateful. How'd you like a nice cup of tea to celebrate?'

Harry grinned. He thought he'd say yes to this offer but when he got to Mr Tinker's house he'd ask for lemonade instead. Lemonade was the drink he liked best. He really loved the fizz.

'Thank you, Mr Tinker, I'd like that,' he said politely, and turned to pick up Cleo's jug.

But it wasn't there.

Chapter Five

HARRY STARED AT the empty spot, unable to believe his eyes. How could the jug just have vanished? He remembered Boris. But Boris couldn't have removed a jug: knocked it over, maybe, but not taken it away! Anyway, Boris had been sent packing by Mr Tinker.

'Hey, Mr Tinker!' Harry wailed. 'Cleo's gone!'

'Eh? What? Don't believe it. Why –'

Harry had had another idea. He

dashed towards the entrance to the lane. Whoever had stolen Cleo might still be in sight. And there, in the distance, heading towards the centre of the village, he could see Jed and Kenny. They seemed to be giggling. They were always giggling together. One would say something and set the other off. They were like that all the time at school. Harry's teacher often said they were like two silly monkeys. But that didn't stop them giggling.

He was sure they were holding something: and he was sure he knew exactly what it was. 'Hey,' he yelled at the top of his voice, 'you've got my goldfish. Bring it back!'

They heard him and they turned round and he could see they really were holding Cleo's jug. But they didn't stop. Instead, they began to run.

'Go get 'em, Harry!' Mr Tinker called. He had come to the main road, too, to see what was happening. 'Show 'em how you dealt with those geese. Thieves is what they are!'

Harry was already running along the pavement. He didn't think, though, that his aeroplane trick would work with Jed and Kenny. They'd probably just stare at him and giggle. Still, that wouldn't

matter if he could get Cleo away from
them. He was beginning to catch up
with them but he wished he could run
faster.

Kenny kept turning round and now
he said something to Jed. Suddenly they
halted and turned to face Harry. They
started giggling again. 'Come and get it,
then, Harry,' they called, holding out
the jug. '*If* you can.'

Harry, too, had stopped, but now he began to walk towards them, wondering how he was going to tackle both boys together. Kenny and Jed began to retreat, walking backwards, still holding the jug out towards him, but looking as if they were ready to run again at any moment. Then Harry noticed what was behind them. Could he just keep their attention for a bit longer . . . ?

'I'm going to get you, and when I get you I'm going to *murder* you two!' he threatened, still advancing, but not too fast. The thieves kept on backing away.

'You couldn't murder a hot dinner,' Kenny called, setting off another fit of giggles.

'I'll mash you up, just wait and see,' Harry promised, still moving forward and praying the two boys wouldn't look round. 'I'll make you scream for mercy.'

'You couldn't –' Jed started to say.

And then, SPLASH! As one, he and Kenny tripped over the rim of the paddling pool, lost balance and went over backwards into the water. The jug flew out of Kenny's grasp and went into the pool, too.

'Cleo!' Harry called, dashing forward now to rescue his goldfish. Now that he'd out-smarted Jed and Kenny he didn't give them another glance. They were soaked to the skin and that silenced their stupid giggles. Now they just wanted to get home and dry off.

Chapter Six

THE POOL WASN'T deep. Once, a year ago, Harry had been pushed in by a couple of boys who were fooling about; and he'd come to no harm, apart from getting soaked. For a few moments he stood on the edge, desperately looking for Cleo. There was no sign of her. She could be anywhere by now. He had to find her, he just *had* to. So in he went.

Too late, he realised he should have taken his shoes and socks off at least.

Already the water was soaking up his trouser legs. Quickly, he bent to roll them up.

'Cleo, Cleo, where are you?' he was calling out, though he knew she couldn't hear him. Even if she could, she wouldn't swim towards him. He knew that. Goldfish just did what they wanted to; nobody could train them or order them about.

Then he saw her! She darted across in front of him. He plunged his hands into the water . . . and missed her. But just to have seen her made him feel better. Now he knew that she was alive and well. She'd come to no harm after being kidnapped by Jed and Kenny. It had been his greatest fear that they'd torment her.

Again Cleo came into view, again Harry lunged for her. This time he

thought he actually touched her but he couldn't be sure. She moved like lightening and the sun was glinting on the water, dazzling him.

'Oh, Cleo, slow down, slow down!' he pleaded. 'Then I'll have a chance of catching you. Then we'll go home again. I'll give you some extra dinner, honest!'

'Harry, Harry, what on earth are you *doing*?' he heard someone calling. 'You'll get soaked if you go in any further.'

When he turned he almost lost his footing. He'd nearly tripped over a branch someone had thrown into the pool. *'Careful!'* the voice called and then he saw that it was Jenny Simpson who was standing by the water's edge.

He liked her because she cut his hair just the way he liked it cut. She owned the hairdressing shop in Main Street where his mother and most of the other people in the village went.

'I'm trying to get my goldfish,' he explained. 'Those horrible boys Jed and Kenny dropped her in the pool, but she seems to slip through my fingers when I try to catch hold of her.'

'I'm not surprised,' Jenny replied. 'It's almost impossible to catch fish with your fingers. Something to do with the way things look in water. They aren't really where you think they are, if you see what I mean. Something to do with the light. Look, hang on, Harry. I've just thought of something that might help. A way of catching your goldfish.'

She looked in her shoulder bag and then held up a package. 'Look at this,' she called. 'Hair nets! New ones. They're quite tough ones, these. I have to keep them in stock for the old ladies who wear them. With a bit of luck, we'll be able to catch your fish in a hair net.'

Harry grinned. 'Thanks, Jenny. That's a great idea.'

'Well, let's hope it works, Harry. Here we go.'

The young hairdresser took off her shoes, ready to wade into the pool. Luckily her legs were bare and she was wearing a mini skirt. She came to stand beside Harry.

'Any luck?' she asked. 'Can you see him?'

'It's a her, not a him,' Harry pointed out. 'Her name is Cleo.'

'Oh, sorry: Cleo,' said Jenny. And at that moment they both saw the goldfish. Jenny stretched out the hairnet with both hands until it was bigger than Harry's own fishing net at home. She gave him one end to hold while she held the other. Together they lowered it into the pool.

'Just keep it still,' Jenny advised.
'With a bit of luck Cleo will swim
straight into the net. Keep it just a little
bit tilted – that's it! As soon as Cleo
touches the net we'll lift it out of the
water and, hey presto, we'll have got
her!'

39

'Like magic,' said Harry.

'Like magic,' Jenny agreed.

They had to be patient. Some people called out to them from the road as they passed by, but Jenny just smiled. It wasn't a time for talking. Then: 'She's coming!' Harry said excitedly.

'Get ready!' Jenny told him.

Like an arrow to its target, Cleo headed into the net. Together, and with perfect timing, Jenny and Harry drew the net upwards – and Cleo was safe.

While Harry dashed ashore for the jug
and dipped it in the pool for some water,
Jenny looked after her. Cleo was
flopping about a bit but she seemed
eager to get back into her jug.

'Well caught, Harry,' Jenny said as
she waded out of the pool and dried her
feet with a large hankie. 'And now
you'd better take her home. I think
she's had enough excitement for one
day.'

'Thanks for all your help,' Harry

replied. He was thinking what he would say to Jed and Kenny at school next day.

He hoped his wet shoes and trousers wouldn't be noticed when he got home. But he needn't have worried. His dad was still watching whizzing cars on the video.

'Well, got over your boredom, have you, you two?' he asked, his eyes still on the screen.

'Yes, thanks. We weren't bored at all, were we, Cleo?' Harry said with a grin.

And Cleo winked.